Grand

by

Dualta Carolan

To my children, **Fintan** and **Caoimhe**.

Also dedicated to **Desmond Little** and **Leo Cosgrove**. I hope your worthy potential becomes fulfilled in other iterations.

Acknowledgments

To **Colleen** and **Nick Thomas**, for your love and support; **Bernadette** and **Seamus Carolan**, for a rich childhood; **Sarah**, my wife and ultimate nemesis; **Mallard Cottage Childcare**, for everything; **Jenny Unthank,** at **Stagecoach**, for your amazing generosity; **Bronach** and **John Carolan**, for the helping hand; **Jason James** and **Gwenan Williams**, for the shed of safety; **Emma Clark**, for support during tough times; **Charlotte Plenty**, for motivational intervention; **Neil Cook**, **David Evans**, **Casey Grenfell** for helpful advice; **Fintan Carolan**, my son, for astute feedback, and **Grove Russell-Allen**, for helping me get across the line.

'pressure... and time...'

Episode 1

'And where we had thought to find an abomination, we shall find a god; where we had thought to slay another, we shall slay ourselves; where we had thought to travel outward, we shall come to the centre of our own existence; where we had thought to be alone, we shall be with all the world.'

JOSEPH CAMPBELL

The Beginning

Quite some time after the birth of creation, a great galaxy sails out upon the expanding universe, its three spirals trailing from one enormous central-disc, suffused with gas and dust that splits its light into sulphuric-yellows, earthy-browns and rusty-reds, along with the faint-white ignitions of newborn stars.

At the furthest stretch of the longest spiral, a particular sun soars, falling into its orbit with fusion raging at its core exploding matter outwards, whilst gravity pulls it back in almost perfect equilibrium.

For its type, however, much larger than the sun that will illuminate your world, this one is approaching the end of its life.

And so, its fiery heart diminishes.

Unable to force matter away, the star collapses inwards, upon itself, waves of convection stampeding throughout, desperately attempting to escape, while thousands of trillions of tonnes crush, further, in...

A blinding flash!

Supernova.

The stricken star ejects streams of energy so fiercely from its poles that it outshines the entirety of the rest of the galaxy. The shockwave is hotter than the sun itself has ever been. Atoms of iron, obliterated from the core, fuse into gold as they are hurled out into interstellar space.

And for a long time, in the great nothingness between galaxies, these atoms of gold attract one another into clumps, some of which form this golden asteroid that is falling and falling and falling and falling and falling…

Until the falling begins to falter.

Then, when the expansion of the Universe, like the lapping edge of a turning tide, breathes its last, up becomes down, down becomes up, and this furthest travelled, most distant object of all, drops back and turns for home, still an eternity from its ultimate destiny.

A journey that is now coming to an end, for here, in my possession, is this final remnant of everything that ever was…

Remembering Ghosts

And now I am a ghost in the world that was, a world where a young girl glitters at the stars, her dark skin shimmers in the moonlight, her hair dances with the breeze.

She skips, similar to how you might skip when playing alone as a child, but here she skips along the ridge of a desert dune on an ancient world, puncturing its silken skin with messy little moonshadows, cascading miniscule avalanches part of the way down the sides.

Here, on this one night of the universe, she wonders at how the tiny grains of sand swirling at her feet can form those mountainous dunes in the distance.

Her father's echoless voice struggles to find her.

'Dariad!'

Eyes firmly on the sky, she trudges towards those oh so distant fires until the camels are snoozing reassuringly, as they should be, beside the tent, and she thanks the stars, as her father always advises, humbly.

Cross-legged in the tent, wearing the black robes of a nomad, Mitian concentrates on the object in his hands. To Dariad, his green eyes appear to contain oceans.

Unbuckling her sandals, she then folds her scarf and lays it beside her bedding.

'Any luck?' she says.

'Not a thing.'

The object, sculpted from ivory, with masterful, intricate carvings all over, mysterious shapes seemingly from an entirely different culture, is out of place here, more reminiscent of the future than the past. To see it, in this desert, in the hands of this lowly merchant, is as strange as it will be to spot an Ancient Greek ceremonial shield propped up against a barn in an Iron Age village. Mitian clasps a tile against the side to hold the sand in while shaking.

'Which way?' she says.

'You're eight, or...'

She smiles. 'I'm nine! You know I am!'

'Nine years? Have you grown so quickly? In which case, I suppose you might as well decide.'

Her hand reaches out to touch it. 'Really?'

'Or you can go to bed...'

'But you've shaken it.'

'Well then,' his smile broadens as the thought occurs. 'It might say something of us both. Which side?'

She considers, her fingers trailing the detail of the carvings. 'This one. Facing me.'

He sets it on the carpet.

'Right.' he says, guiding her in front. 'Take it away and say what comes to mind.'

As she removes the tile, fine sand spills out.

'A sea of sand.' she whispers.

Inside, twelve small sculptures protrude from the back in three columns of four.

'You've seen this before, haven't you?'

'Once or twice. But I don't know what any of it means.'

'What do you think about when

you look at the idols, from the way the sand has settled around them?'

She looks at the figure to the top-left, a snake. 'Doesn't each one connect to the three beneath? Each stops the sand from reaching the next. But if I'd done it differently, the rows wouldn't be the same…'

'Don't think so much. What do you feel? What does your gut tell you?'

'Well, I said about it being like the sea, but everyone knows that.'

'And yet we are not at sea. This is the desert. Could be important. What else?'

Dariad imagines her father drowning in a sea of sand, flailing desperately in a turmoil of dust as the desert drags him in. She feels as if this is the last night she will ever see him.

But she also senses something of a new beginning, like the time at the top of that cliff, when the thought occurred that she could, if she really wanted to, allow herself to fall to the rocks below. In that moment, a sense of freedom had washed over her, just before she stepped back, frightened not to be able to resist the impulse.

Her voice doesn't dare mention a word of this, for fear of its coming true.

'What do you see, father?'

'No, you first. Before long, you'll know the positions of the idols, which is why you weren't supposed to touch it. The first readings are the most pure.

'What's this?'

'A tiger. Remember the forest, up north?'

'Even more vast than the desert?'

'That's the one.'

'Need to see it to believe that.'

'Three times larger, I've been told. Well, a tiger is the biggest, scariest, most terrifying thing living there. If you ever saw one, you still wouldn't believe.'

'Why? Have you?'

'No... But your mother did.'

'Really? What was it like?'

'Beautiful. Powerful.' Mitian's eyes fall into memory but recover before she notices.

'They're ferocious hunters, tigers. You can't see it here, but they have this gorgeous fur, all golden and white, with sleek black stripes, and two long sharp teeth jutting up from the bottom row.' He points. 'Each as long as this finger. A few years back, I held a hide in these very hands - so soft! But your mother, as young as you are now - she witnessed one in all its glory.'

'How?'

'Well, back then life wasn't so easy. Your grandfather left Yojaief and took the family north seeking better opportunity. They were trekking through the jungle with a larger group, arriving into a clearing, when your mother emerged to find all who had come before her stopped still.

'And there he was, a huge tiger, standing at the centre like a king, his massive eyes considering whether to make an example of trespassers onto his territory. But when his gaze fell upon her, his eyes sprang alert and he stepped forward with his paw tracing the air ready to run.'

'He attacked?'

'Her heart was thumping in her ears, she told me, but no - he hesitated, and then became relaxed, and then he just stood there, growling tenderly.'

'I don't understand.'

'He seemed to *know* her... Your

grandfather said the same. For him, it was as if there was something wondrous about her that no one else could see, as if he had cared for her but she had been lost, and he had wondered for those intervening years what became of her.

'Now content he need no longer worry, he sauntered the opposite way, pausing to look one last time before melting into the trees, never to be seen again.

'After, when they breathed out and were laughing, sharing the fear they had felt, your mother noticed each and every parent holding a blade, so absolutely silently had they unsheathed them, and it was a long time before they were put back.

'That moment, she told me, when his eyes met with hers, was the most magical of her life. He moved, she said, as if power and grace had fallen madly in love. I loved the way she used to say that.'

'She'd tell it like that?'

'She would.'

'And did she ever find out?'

Mitian's eyebrows wrinkle in confusion.

'What was wondrous about her?'

'She did.'

'What was it?'

He smiles. 'You.'

There is a silence that follows such an utterance, but then there is the curiosity of a child inspired to know more.

'How does a tiger live?"

'From what your mother said, they do as they please. But I have heard stories over the years from friends who sighted them or heard from others who did. When hunting, they say, a tiger creeps, so slowly, but then halts, frozen like a statue, eyes on you like the sun. You glance about but dismiss the feeling that something is there, watching, waiting, continuing its approach once you've relaxed and gone back to your grazing.'

'That's absolutely terrifying! The thought of something watching that's about to eat you.'

'You're mother believed there was more muscle on its head than she had on her entire body. So now imagine all that muscle taking a single tentative step, body shaped like an arrow, every joint and muscle poised to pounce... you glance once more, but there's no danger... the statue is hidden amongst the grass...'

Mitian raises his claws and her eyes widen with delight. She glances about for a means of escape.

'Your heart flushes as you turn...'

She turns. 'No, father!'

'To escape...'

She bolts, laughing yet remaining within range as he rushes in.

'Aah! No!'

He pounces, tickling her, and Dariad's heart is filled with torturous happiness.

'Father!'

'But it's too late!'

They catch their breaths together with laughter reigniting infectiously between them, and then there are sighs of recovery.

But she remembers the object and returns with renewed focus. The tiger tops the middle of the three rows of four, the central column above the lump of sand. The tiger's eyes are filled with sand. Underneath this is a man. Sand covers his head but the rest of him remains untouched. She is reminded of her father. Below is an elephant and, finally, a star. The star doesn't have anything on it whatsoever.

She is overwhelmed by a feeling of relaxation, of letting go.

'My first thought is that bad things are going happen, but then I think I'm wrong. I'm actually really...' She yawns. '...tired. Is that right, what I said?'

'Good enough. Time for bed. We'll be setting off early. I'll tell you on the way.'

She kisses him and climbs into bed. From under her blanket, she watches as he sips his tea, those green eyes reflecting upon the object.

∞∞∞

A tender circling on the back of her hand falls away and she is shaking, or being shaken. She reaches to wipe away a tear, and now her arms stretch out in response to the gentle shaking of her shoulders.

'Get up.'

'A little longer...'

'Dariad.'

'What's wrong?'

'Get dressed - quickly! We have to leave. You awake?

'Yes...'

'Now!'

She sits up with his back disappearing out, leaving her with a child's instinct to catch up. She dresses, at the same time stuffing some clothes into a sack, not yet fully awake, before following after.

Outside, in the blue pre-dawn, Mitian fastens supplies to two of the camels, with the third and fourth standing ready. Of the final pair, one opens his eyes and closes them again.

Making herself useful, Dariad goes to rouse him.

'Leave them, and leave the shelter as it is. Bring the smaller one. Pack food for a week and any clothes you might need. I've done your water. Here.' He pats the waterskin in front of the saddle. He looks up.

'What's happening?'

Without a word, he harnesses the third camel and reins it to the second.

'Why are we -'

'Do as you're told!'

Having never been spoken to by him like this, Dariad runs inside and packs some food and anything else that might be useful, but when she returns and ties these to the beast, it is as if the wind has picked up, the air heavy, like before a storm on the northern plains. Are her senses playing tricks?

Mitian finishes reining the fourth animal and is waiting when she pulls the last bag tight.

'Ready?'

'I'll pack for you.'

He crouches down, capturing her hands in his. 'I'm staying here.'

At first there is no reaction, but then, as her eyes make sense of it, her bottom lip pushes upward.

'But why?'

He brushes his thumb across her cheek, as if to hold back her tears. 'I'm sorry for shouting. You've done nothing wrong. And to be honest, I'm not even sure what I've seen. But I have to know you're safe, as far away from me as possible. Don't worry - when the time has passed, I'll find you in Yojaief. But until then you're on your own.

Listen - until I meet you in the city, you must never come back, no matter what happens. Do you promise?'

'Yes.'

'Say it.'

'I promise!'

He holds her close. 'Don't worry - I'll be with you and all this will have been nothing. Go to your uncle.' He picks her up and hugs her. 'I love you *more* than the world."

She remembers last night's terrifying imagining. This might really be that last time she sees him.

'Please don't do this! Let me stay!'

But she is being raised up onto the camel and then he is tying her sand-scarf gently about her neck. As he does so, from nowhere, that beautiful broadening of his smile surprises her into one her own, like the sun bursting from the darkest clouds.

'What?'

'It isn't all bad, you know.' he says, double-checking her sword by her side. 'The bones. There's good too - I just can't see it.'

His hand reaches trailing through her hair, and then her clothing is being checked in the way a parent checks things when there is nothing more they can think to do to protect a child leaving alone.

With that, and a firm pat to the hindquarters of the beast, she moves away.

'Stay alive,' he shouts, his smile turning to fear. 'Stay strong. Get as far away as you can!'

Sea of Sand

So Dariad now journeys west-by-south in the direction of Yojaief, barely noticing the dawn unfurl into the sky or even, a little later, the Sun glancing over the horizons of the dunes, casting their majesty in profile.

The sky, hazy and pale, still retains faint traces of clouds carried from the sea during the night, but she doesn't pay much attention to that either, or even the illusory sunsets and sunrises encountered while trekking down dunes and climbing from the shadows of those coming after, which usually fill her with delight.

Dariad understands that this is all happening, without question, for her own good, and for a time, as the Sun slides over the slopes, she is buoyed by the feeling of still being under his protection, as well his faith in her to reach the city on her own. She has imagined being able to, but it's nice to know he thinks so too.

And the shadows pursue now all the while, elongated across the train of beasts, across their freshly made tracks, catching hold of each foot padding down onto the sand, yet darting back into the wake of crumbling footprints when it is swept through with hoofed-toes skirting the surface, for the awaiting shadow to catch hold once more upon touching down.

As the day wears on, she continues to be oblivious to this rhythm of movement, and to the shortening of the shadows beneath. Her heart feels so confused by the contrast between her father's noble intention and the decision to send her away.

To Dariad, in the same way as it might be for you, her father is the first and greatest of all gods. In fact, as far back as she dares to remember, her father and mother were *both* that first god, ever-present in her faintest cherished memories, holding her close, whispering that they would always be there.

That was, until the morning her father sat beside her to explain how the other half of her world had journeyed to a far off distant land, and that, though her mother wanted to more than anything in the world, she would never be coming home. The most feminine presence ever to exist simply disappeared, her touch never to be felt, her voice never to be heard again.

As time crept by and Dariad came to understand the permanence of her loss, a powerful rage emerged into being, etching itself into the faultlines of her heart. Of course, it wasn't her mother's fault. Dariad knows that. How could it be? Her mother didn't choose to die, did she? But alas, the anger resides within regardless, sometimes exhibiting itself as courage or resilience, but it is really the pain of knowing that someone you love can be lost forever, no matter how much your world revolves around them.

While her mother faded into mystery, an absent god to be longed for from afar, he who remained became transformed into a vulnerable mortal man for, if she could die, it followed that he could too.

Dariad's good fortune is that she has come to respect her father much more for who he is than the god she thought him to be. Nothing in world can match being loved without limit by such a person but, being mortal, his safety can only ever be certain when he is holding her close and whispering that everything is going to be all right.

Now that she has envisioned his doom and he has been startled enough to stay where he is, it seems that he might also betray her, without meaning to, and disappear forever.

Her eyebrows scrunch together and her eyes close in a final attempt to hold back the floods, but she is starting to cry, with all her worry, anguish and pain bursting forth.

Such a waste of fluid is a sinful act, so Dariad convinces herself that all will be well, but then, whilst being carried along, she imagines how he must have seen the same as her in the bones and her mind circles back, caught within the whirlpool, each time teetering close to sanity before being pulled into the certainty of his demise. A sigh of grief then emanates out, turning to a moan, that can only be subdued by tears.

The head-shadow of the lead-camel, however, the one on which she sits, has bobbed its way into her field of vision and this, along with the swaggering shadow of his neck, induces her into a daze, providing respite from the madness within. But then her own shadow mercilessly narrows the gap of light, and when the two merge, the spell is shattered, reawakening her awareness that she is here, all alone, without her father, cast out, vulnerable.

Having travelled this way throughout her childhood, she is as intimate with such shadows as you might be with the final curves and gradients of a long journey home. Had they not found one another within fifty breaths of doing so, her mind would have jolted awake to estimate how far she had strayed from her course, and how best to divert across to rejoin it.

Her renewed suffering, therefore, is not the fault of the shadows. The blame lies with this nightmare for being real.

She halts the train at the top of the last dune and takes a mouthful from the waterskin. Her father would, no doubt, instruct her to have some more, and so being the loving daughter, she complies with her imaginary-father's wishes, further reminded that he isn't here, the silence of his absence starkly more apparant.

The plains are laid out invitingly ahead, but the air is beginning to chill, the sky is losing its lustre, night is closing in. Darkness will be upon her before the shelter is even up.

She leads them around in a circle, down into the valley between these somewhat smaller dunes, before ascending up the leeward side of the next, out of the breeze. Though Dariad is well aware she has trouble leaving without him, camping here for the night is still the correct decision, much better sheltered than on the plains with its shrieking draughts and hard earth, especially should a sandstorm hit as one easily might without warning, when reaching the highest point above the piercing sand is paramount.

With a gentle pressing of her foot against his neck, she is angled downwards by the camel until he lurches back to bring her level again, lowering his hind-quarters and settling to the sand.

Now on her own two feet, she stands looking back, desperately hoping that her father might emerge from the last of the mirages.

∞∞∞

Mitian is here, however, lying in the tent, day-dreaming of the time his grandmother finally answered about the bones, her presence so powerful and reassuring that surely she would always be there.

'All right! I'll tell you!' she had smiled bittersweetly just then. 'Once upon a time, as impossible as it might seem, I was your age, younger even, when I asked my grandfather that same question - he'd be your great-great-grandfather, may the gods remember him. And do you know what? He didn't know either! So let's just you and I agree it's been in the family for a *long* time.'

Mitian remembers her smile lingering as she sipped from her basan and then turned to the elders to discuss more serious matters. He regrets not having posed one question about his great-great-grandfather, not even to ask for his name, and in Mitian's soul he hopes that the gods remember his grandmother as he does.

If something happens here, the bones will disappear, lost forever in the sand, or worse - be stolen away. If only he had given it to Dariad to take with her.

His flesh relaxes in surrender as he emerges into the heat. With it being so late he has neglected to wear his black robes, which usually absorb the sunlight with the air against his skin remaining cool, but he's happy enough with these white ones he has on, more comfortable for sitting around in the tent all day.

With nothing else to do, he checks the sturdiness of the shade under which the camels rest. It won't at this point make any difference to the animals, but Mitian must conserve his energy before taking it down.

In this part of the world the transformation from day to night is as swift as the flicking of one of your switches.

Here, however, it is the gods who flick such switches, and only when they have done so can he remove the shade with little effort. For now, the air is still so humid that his hand wipes sweat from his face without him even noticing.

Out of nowhere, a voice is heard.

'Hello!'

Mitian shades his eyes from the sun to discover a stranger, short and stocky, huffing and puffing his way down the slope leading his train of three camels.

'Safety and blessings upon you!' he smiles, catching his breath. 'My name is Fasan.'

Mitian remains impassive. 'Safety and blessings on those who deserve them.'

'An important point I'm sure but, to be honest, I'm just relieved to hear another voice, deserving or otherwise. That's my blessing - eight days and nights without a soul for company. I'm not intruding?'

The man's smile meets his eyes.

'You're welcome here, my friend. I'm heading for Yojaief and was about to give thanks and rest, but a decent conversation would be a great improvement. I am Mitian.'

Fasan slaps him on the shoulder. 'Excellent!' He begins unbuckling the animals. 'We'll have basan and trade tales. To whom do you give thanks?'

As with expectation, Mitian offers his waterskin. 'That's for me to know.'

'Ah - I like you already!' The man takes a gulp and hands it back. 'Thank you. Wise men keep such things to themselves. You know what?' He turns, searching through his bags. 'I've been saving a bottle of marlash...'

'Really?'

'I have the feeling, now is the time.'

As high up and as far away as can be seen, an enormous mass of light smashes into the blue, as if thrown by a god from the heavens, and they stand watching in awe, children realising the fiction of their games, transfixed by the sight of it blazing towards them, a mountain of white light shedding parts of itself, its luminosity drowning the world in a flash of darkness as it rages silently overhead, and then a mighty deafening roar blasts down, drowning their senses as it thunders out of sight beyond the dune.

A dull thump becomes followed by trembling, the earth now alive with pain, the desert writhing in shock, the animals calling and braying in deep grunts of despairing song, and the two men are thrown aside like dolls with sand sweeping over them.

Pulling himself out of it, Mitian's heart fills with dread. The source of all his love must face this terrible wrath by herself, and there is nothing he can do to help.

∞∞∞

Clambering from the sand about twenty paces from where she just stood, with her body aching from the jolt that sent her flying, Dariad staggers to the first beast and tries to calm him when she sees, starting in the distance, the desert rising like a wave, as if being hurled into the sky.

She steps back, her hand pulling her sword from its sheath. Then finally managing to wrestle away her gaze, she turns, swinging the blade through the reins connecting the animals, pulling the first one down and mounting.

Without signal, it is up and away.

'Hut!' she shouts, pressing her feet hard into his neck, striking his shoulder with the broadside of her sword. 'Come on! Hut!'

The world dims hurriedly as darkness envelops the Sun. The deep thumping of her heartbeat is overwhelming, like a crashing drum trying to escape from her chest, along with some kind of sensation of an almighty cracking and buckling deep underground.

A molten glow hisses into the sand, with another just to the side, and more and more raining all around. She can hear the moaning and wailing of the animals galloping ahead, barely picking one of them from the murk that now enshrouds her, when a stone smacks its head and it tumbles to a stop as she flies past, coughing, pulling up her scarf to breathe.

She glances up in a vain effort to dodge anything that might hit her but, deep down, she knows she is powerless.

And then everything slows, all fear disappearing as her mind shifts into a trance. Eyes sparkling, she can feel the heat of her breath against the fabric, see the debris coming from above, hear the grunting of the animal as he gallops down the long slope of the last dune, unbalanced by the gamble to run as fast as possible.

Showers of sand hang in the air, made golden by what remains of the light. Soft tears slope and split around the grains caked to Dariad's cheeks by the wind... the animal's muscles thrust beneath with a gasping breath for every push as the two of them hive with life...

All this, she perceives, like a dance

in a dream, to the slow and steady rhythm of her heart…

Birth

West of Yojaief, far across the ocean, there lies an undiscovered land, except by those born within.

Here, my father flies through cities of light, world after world, system after system, so fast that the colours of the galaxies combine like rainbows being torn apart.

There is something he is after.

In stillness he floats with no sound, no light, nothing at all. He is lost, powerless, doomed, like a fly about to be smashed by the hand of a giant. The certainty of annihilation is so overpowering that he roars, and yet makes no sound.

But a point of light blossoms like a ripple from the blackness and he feels raptures of joy, the same joy from before this... all this... but then the light shrinks back to be replaced by a tidal wave sent forth to drown that joy...

My father breaks forwards, sitting up in bed, shouting for me.

'Hiatim!'

While he recovers, a hand reaches from beside, gathering back his hair.

'It was just a dream.'

His memory can't quite catch hold to look at it so he turns to her lying there, barely visible in the dark, with me nestled by her breast.

'Is he...'

'Sound asleep.'

Lying back with her arm coming to a rest across his stomach, he turns to face her, caressing her skin, running his fingers through her hair.

'You?'

'Fine.' She says. 'Tired.'

He stays until she falls asleep, watching us both a while before getting up and going outside.

That dream. If he could just remember.

Earlier tonight, not long after holding me in his arms the first time, he stood here on this hillside outside our home, listening to the whispering of the trees, wondering if my grandfather felt the same when faithful to the light of a new soul.

Lost somewhere between the darkness of the forest and the crispness of the sky, a bright flash pulled him into the moment, illuminating the outlines of the trees as it shot from behind, sailing across the sky.

A star only falls when a god dies, to be reborn as a mortal, to see this world anew before ascending again to their rightful place.

My father remembers my grandfather telling him this, long ago.

The Nomad

It is strange to discover the desert so wounded, especially for two men who have grown up knowing it so well.

In nomadic culture, the sharing of songs and stories with those met along the way, of recitations of great adventure, supreme acts of survival, or the most marvellous yarns to surprise companions into laughter, is the single most important tradition of all. When the sun rises each morning, it unveils the desert reborn, beginning again with its markings erased and little sign that anyone ever existed here. So without the nomads and their stories, the desert would have no memory.

Here and now, however, as they make their way amongst the scars, the wounds are deepening. The desert *is* telling a story, more epic perhaps than any told before, albeit a tale unfinished, much too grand as yet to be understood.

Yesterday evening, when that monstrosity flashed overhead and out of sight behind the dunes, Fasan was reaching for his clay bottle, the one holding his beloved marlash.

Similar to wine in many respects, marlash is said to truly warm the soul. It is so rare, however, that the only one he knows to have tasted it is Jensu, the giver of the gift, grateful for a favour not nearly equal in value, with Fasan having offered to delay receipt of payment for his wares, which unbeknownst to him had allowed his friend to continue trading.

A year later, while paying what

was owed, and with Fasan putting the money away without counting, Jensu placed the bottle in his hands, not letting go until his friend understood the importance of his act of kindness, and that the longer one waited before drinking, the better the taste.

Upon releasing his grip, Jensu also stated definitively that wine doesn't come close to describing the pleasure, with marlash being so much more powerful and smooth and elegant, not to mention, of course, its other mysterious effects.

Since that day, he has found himself nodding agreeably when sitting by a fire on a cold night, as a fellow has declared marlash to be nothing but a myth, a rumour sprung to life out of a story told in some inn by an old pirate unhappy with his wine, all the while Fasan glancing in the direction of his clay bottle, satisfied that his beloved marlash is too valuable to be wasted delighting this man.

And so, until last night, he has carried it around for years, waiting for just such a moment as when his eyes set themselves on Mitian. Instantly Fasan knew that here was a kindred spirit, a man whose heart was as connected to the desert as his own, to whom traditional nomadic life came naturally, and who understood the value of a good story.

Fasan has since realised how right he was, with both having made their way to Yojaief as young men, each using his knowledge of the desert to trade in goods across its vast swathes.

Fastened to Mitian's camels are bolts of silk, both beasts overloaded somewhat due to the departure of the others. Then there are the spices and scents searching out Mitian's senses from Fasan's train. Once sold, the profits might purchase a measure of gold or gems, highly sought after in the east, or salt, just as priceless here in the desert and a guarantee of safe passage along the way.

Regardless of the greatness of the city, with so much in common, it's a surprise they've never met in all these years. Then again, it wouldn't be the first time.

The fragrances wafting through his scarf remind Mitian of both daughter *and* wife, of their grace and power, one lost forever, the other...

Fasan points. 'There!'

His heart leaps, but no - not Dariad. The worst of the carnage has emerged from the haze, a massive area of the desert now ash-grey in colour.

He lowers his scarf with a deep intake of breath. 'Have you seen anything like it?

'Not in my lifetime.' Fasan says.

'That's were we'll start. For now, though, we must make camp.'

'Another hour.'

Fasan pulls back. 'You're taking chances. You know better.'

But Mitian continues on.

'She was a day ahead. She's missed it!'

'She'd have taken her time.'

'That might be, but we aren't getting any further tonight. Searching in the dark won't help her. That, right there, is an hour we don't have!'

Mitian halts, becoming a statue.

The sun has fallen out of sight, its light casting from behind the horizon, the terrain losing its distinction.

The statue sighs. 'We make camp.'

∞∞∞

Dariad lies quiet and unmoving.

The morning sun *has* made itself apparent. Her eyes *have* opened in response. But she still hasn't moved. She is just lying on the ground, cheek against the dirt, confused to be alive.

And now she shifts, wincing, shaking off her blanket of sand, sitting up to better see the debris scattered on the plains, with the wind already clearing the lighter dust from between the rocks, but she feels so light-headed, her vision so bleached, that she isn't quite sure what she's looking at.

Her fingers reach instinctively, exploring the congealed cut beneath the tangle on her head. Maybe that's why the morning Sun seems so painfully bright, and she wonders if that gallop down the final dune actually happened. The memory bears such a resemblance to other nightmares that have stayed with her; an all powerful force closing in, with no possibility of escape, followed by a vague awakening.

Behind, however, when she turns, the dune towers ten times higher than before. She considers what her fate might have been, had she not escaped it, and shivers at flash-imaginings of smothering.

She swallows to conjure spit but none appears, with the effort worsening her terrible panging thirst. If she isn't careful, it will come to possess her.

That, she *has* witnessed before, when her father fought with a man just to save him, his madness so far-gone that he was walking around in circles, jabbering nonsense, unable to consider reason, but was then so grateful a few weeks later when they called to see how he was. Dariad was suprised at how different he seemed with his senses regained. At the time, she had thought it better, with all of his curses and threats, to leave him where he was to die in the sand, but she was glad her father had seen through all that.

The thirst is already whispering to begin for the city, but she won't be goaded, not yet anyway. If she doesn't go up and survey what has happened, it will haunt her for the rest of her life, and Dariad already understands how lasting regret can be.

Very quickly, she falls into a routine of short climbs followed by long rests. She is a determined soul, hardened to this life, but that doesn't make much difference when a person is hungry and thirsty with energy draining from their muscles. As she hoists and scrapes and traverses herself up one section after another, she begins to suspect she was lying there on the gound for more than just the night.

A day at the mercy of the worst of the heat might explain her sorry state, including the throbbing in her head, but when she thinks of how she might have been lying in such a way as to take the sun on her face, or if this massive slope hadn't been here to provide shade, she sighs at her luck.

Eventually, by pure force of will, she reaches the top, the very edge of a wide plateau sloping away for miles. Far down, it seems as though a giant has gouged a handful from the desert, with Dariad standing at periphery of where it was thrown.

She remembers being down there somewhere thinking things couldn't get any worse, praying for her father to appear so she wouldn't be alone without him. Now she prays the opposite, that he stayed far behind where he was.

The thought of losing him almost causes her legs to give way. It is a despair from which she could never recover. But she can't think like this - he'd have known what to do. He always knows.

Dariad would gladly break her oath to search him out but she'll be lucky to make the city herself, a promise that can't be broken. To do so would be to insult him.

The closer she comes as she slides back down, checking over her shoulder for fear of the entire mass collapsing on top of her, the longer the journey ahead seems to appear. With a camel for travel and shade, she might make it in a day or two but, with no water, no food, nothing to protect her from the sun, she'll simply have to keep walking and hope for the best.

Something, however, across the face of this enormous, misshapen dune of debris, catches her eye. At first glance, it appears to be some kind of moss or root, thrown about during the chaos, but Dariad soon realises what she is actually looking at - the underside of the beast, curving towards the base of his neck.

Struggling across the incline, she drops to her knees, grasping the sand from around him, working her hands up to the muzzle, feeling around to discern his posture.

Her stomach wretches at the stench, but her thirst fights desperately against vomiting.

As she acclimatises, her hands pause on his neck, shocked that such a thing, so alive as they fought together for survival, can now be so lifeless and still. She considers the majesty of his achievement, how powerful and decisive he was in saving her life.

'Thank you!' she whispers.

When the moment passes, she scoops the sand from around him, wrestling a bag out of the way, then levering the waterskin to and fro underneath until it shifts free, and she gulps it down, the finest water ever tasted.

She sits for a while, eating some chevon, giving the water a chance to work its magic, gulping when she feels like it, until she is somewhat like herself again. Once so, she finds a second waterskin and some clothes, much to be appreciated when the temperature drops tonight.

And so, with a determined breath, she starts walking toward Yojaief.

∞∞∞

The destruction is unnerving, with the land rising up and reaching out, possibly even to the plains. At the low point, surely the location of the impact, our two friends peer from the top of a slope leading steeply underground into what seems to be a large trench running below the surface.

At least, that's what they think it might be.

Several openings are spaced ahead in a line along the ground, seeming to fall into the same cavernous area, although looking from any of these seems too much of a risk; the earth or rock around them might collapse at any time.

The slope is likely where it struck, melting the sand while tearing through, with the molten mass falling in but hardening before meeting in the middle to leave the emptiness between. The desert dips increasingly into the sides along this valley of perforations, then rising immensely thereafter until the plateau. Such a enormous expanse of sand shunted forwards, so effortlessly.

'We should see what's down there.'

Mitian glances almost to the spot where Dariad has just been standing on the plateau, and back to the trench. He nods, 'We'll need to be quick.'

Taking care not to slip, they clamber down until finding a relatively level footing and head towards a hollow fifty paces further in, beyond the pillars of light shining from above. Fasan wipes his sweat away, shocked that the air is still more humid than the desert at its most fierce. With his scarf up, he breathes through his mouth to avoid the smell of bitter-charcoal, but it lingers on his tongue.

This, as well as the haunting silence permeating everywhere, causes a terrifying thought to occur.

'Could something be alive down here?'

They halt, in unison, listening for danger, startled by the possibility of predators. Something monstrous could easily lurk there in the darkness.

Such a deafening quiet has instilled caution into the hearts of two men perfectly suited to lying alone during nights in blustering winds with enormous dunes towering invisibly over, an experience which on its own would fill others with dread.

At some time during your childhood, you might find yourself lying in bed unable to sleep, reflecting upon earlier in the evening when you were running around with everyone in the excitement. You might even congratulate yourself, thinking about it, on your inspired choice of hiding place!

But still lingering, your imagination will run with the thought.

And there it is, the closet door left

open! Why did you have to go and do that? What if someone is there now, maybe even a monster, watching from the darkness, waiting until you sleep?

You might begin to believe that such an evil presence, so newly born, really does lie beyond the light shining from the hallway, watching from the dark recesses of that closet, daring you to jump from your bed and turn on the lights to be sure. You might be about to do exactly that when the suspicion dawns...

Will that make the monster real?

So to avoid becoming the one to be whispered about in scary stories, you lie there terrified and alone, staring at an empty closet, failing to convince yourself that there's nothing truly to fear.

As it evolves to affect you in this way, the same feeling will have been felt by hundreds of thousands of generations who have descended through time to your lying there in that bed. It has already been felt by a similar number who have lived out their lives until this moment Mitian now endures.

Real predators, hungry for the flesh of these children, waited in the darkness while mothers and fathers, as caring and worried as Mitian is now, warned and scolded them through epochs of nights to remain close to the flames of the fires protecting them.

Children are children, however, with many still curious and courageous enough to venture away, never to be seen again, with fathers holding mothers back from rushing out to helpless screams of agony being cut-short, lest they suffer the same fate.

Of course, such a terrible event would never be forgotten by any children present, and they, in their turn as mothers and fathers, would warn and scold and terrify their young.

With the horrible imaginings that saved their lives when they were young, they would concoct fairytales with beasts lying in wait amidst the woods, or monsters dragging innocents from water's edges, or into caves, with countless children managing, despite all this, to disappear, and so on, with imaginations terrifying enough to ensure survival growing steadily more powerful, generation by generation, transforming wolves into demons, bears into monsters, filling any dark emptiness with whatever personal horrors might stop a person venturing there.

But by the time Mitian is standing here considering this awaiting darkness, he has spent his last nine years reassuring Dariad of the harmlessness of such thoughts. He isn't even sure why he has chosen to stop now, although the abounding silence is the reason, the quietest yet experienced. During all those generations, such a silence meant one thing - a predator so fearsome that all life had fled.

Ultimately, however, Mitian is so used to making light of such imaginings that it's difficult to be frightened of anything not right in front of his face.

So he shakes his head. 'It was hot enough to melt the sand. Nothing survived down here.' He then repeats the words routinely spoken to his daughter. 'Just our imaginations playing tricks.'

Fasan doesn't have children. 'Regardless,' he decides. 'I'll go no further without a weapon.'

As he scurries back, Mitian's thoughts are left festering in the dark. If only he kept Dariad close. She shouldn't have been on her own. Sending her off like that put her in harm's way. She might have been right here when it...

He shudders.

She'll be waiting in the city when I get there!

It's not the darkness that scares him, but the idea of knowing for certain that she has been lost.

Where there is uncertainty, with the outcome as yet unknown, hope remains, the hope that she is safe, walking through the city gates right now, the closest witness to that flashing chaos in the sky everyone's so excited about. People are asking questions, with her answers proving how wondrous and brave and intelligent she is.

No - she'll be worried about him, something he hasn't yet considered. She won't want to talk to anyone, and she won't have gotten that far yet anyway. If she survived, she'll still be on her way...

If she survived...

If...

For him, the "If" has become the most terrible flip of a coin, a gamble that can't be lost. *If* so, once revealed, the other outcome, the one engraved with hope, can never again be turned to face the sky.

He has witnessed such hope lingering in the hearts of others, transforming into a curse, haunting them to desire to *know the worst*, so they might finally let go.

Mitian vows never to desire such a truth.

She'll be waiting in Yojaief!

No longer able to contend with such thoughts, he presses ahead towards the opening, spreading his palm against the boiled-dry wall, sliding it along and taking in its smoothness. Grains of sand crunch underfoot, echoing around with Fasan's loudening footsteps as he arrives with gasping breath.

The hilt of a sword is placed in Mitian's hand. 'Thought you might want it.'

'Thank you.' It feels a lot better in his grasp than strapped to the side of a camel. That much is true.

'This atmosphere, Mitian, I've known nothing like it.'

Mitian passes into the shadows. 'Me neither.'

Now at the entrance, eyes adapting to the dark, an area of blackness becomes illuminated across the way.

'Another opening?'

Mitian steps through. 'One way to find out.'

'I... I'll wait here.'

Staring intently at the second opening, for that is what it must be, he approaches with his hand reaching out, ready to pass through... But this chamber is larger than it first appeared. The area of blackness clarifies to become a rock, twelve paces long, with its base welded diagonally to the ground.

Realising how central it is, Mitian circles respectfully. He can't see the chamber-walls, but their texture, the roughness of their touch, suggests only violence. In his bones he is sure that all of the force to move the desert emanated from here - from this.

When he reaches the opposite end of the chamber, its shape becomes clear against the opening, jutting from the ground like the head of a spear thrown from distance, and Mitian wonders if this beautiful shard can possibly be all that is left of what came overhead two nights ago.

'It's a rock!' he says. 'A big one.'

'Nothing to fear then?'

He approaches, laying his hand on it. Cold and smooth, like marble. 'It's not warm or damaged. Seems out of place in all this...'

A funny feeling comes over him, as if his blood is running as cold as that which he has touched. His hand pulls away but won't be released. Something is emerging, flowing directly into Mitian's mind. He can hear the thoughts of something other than himself, something brutal, something... innocent.

Through his clenched teeth, there is only a strained whisper. 'Get... away!'

'What?'

Mitian's other hand sets itself against the stone, with the strange consciousness streaming in even more rapidly.

'Mitian?'

But Mitian's sense of himself is disappearing, as if he is falling asleep against the might of his will. He holds on to his love... for a... daughter...

Memories sweep through him... the birth of Dariad... the hope in her that remained with the sorrow... Memories of his mother, once vague and distant, are now fresh as if he is a child again, clumsily feeling around, being lifted towards her... the smell of Tasian as he speaks of others too feeling as if they came into the world from nothing, and who also struggled to understand... To the West of Yojaief, Tasian's back as he quietly contemplates the great ocean... so majestic and at one with the world that Mitian believes his father to be a god... such hopeful sadness...

Dariad's lesson will be blunt.

The same quiet, hopeful sadness rushes through Mitian's being, and he is gone.

'Mitian?'

Mitian turns to face him with his eyes white, as if light is shining from them.

As Fasan tries to make sense of it, a force takes hold and he turns to run but, mid-step, evaporates into a faint vapor, which rushes into the body of the man who was once Mitian. The Nomad steps over Fasan's clothes and sword, back through the pillars of light until reaching the foot of the slope, but his body weakens, falling hard against it.

A camel appears at the lip, disintegrating into a swirling cloud that floods back to The Nomad, streaming between his fingers and, in their shock, the remaining camels bolt out-of-sight, galloping past the trench, up toward the plateau.

As he looks around at the trench and then up at the sky, the Nomad's attention is caught by the grains of sand at his feet. He crouches to gather some, balancing them on his palm, watching them roll around. When they fall, he catches them between fingers and thumb. Now conscious that these are his, he drops the sand, staring at his hands, wriggling his fingers, opening and closing his fists, astounded at his control over them.

Using his legs to stand, he climbs the incline to the lip and emerges into the desert, but stumbles again to the ground.

The camels, still running, froth dripping from their mouths, disintegrate mid-gallop, with their saddles, harnesses, bolts of silk, fragrances, supplies, waterskins and basan smashing to the ground, along with the bones, and Fasan's beloved bottle of marlash.

The Nomad feels his strength return, but he has learned his lesson - moving makes him weak.

There'll be no more movement.

To be continued.

***Episode 2** coming soon.*

https://www.facebook.com/quantumparadoxism/

Printed in Poland
by Amazon Fulfillment
Poland Sp. z o.o., Wrocław